SKOKIE PUBLIC LIBRARY

3 1232 01085 2897

D0801439

MARYA KHAN

✽ AND THE ✽
FABULOUS JASMINE GARDEN

AMULET BOOKS • NEW YORK

MARYA KHAN

❀ AND THE ❀

FABULOUS JASMINE GARDEN

written by
SAADIA FARUQI

illustrated by
ANI BUSHRY

PUBLISHER'S NOTE: This is a work of fiction. Names, characters, places, and incidents are either the product of the author's imagination or used fictitiously, and any resemblance to actual persons, living or dead, business establishments, events, or locales is entirely coincidental.

Cataloging-in-Publication Data has been applied for and may be obtained from the Library of Congress.

ISBN 978-1-4197-6118-8

Text © 2023 Saadia Faruqi
Illustrations © 2023 Ani Bushry
Book design by Deena Fleming

Published in 2023 by Amulet Books, an imprint of ABRAMS. All rights reserved. No portion of this book may be reproduced, stored in a retrieval system, or transmitted in any form or by any means, mechanical, electronic, photocopying, recording, or otherwise, without written permission from the publisher.

Printed and bound in U.S.A.
10 9 8 7 6 5 4 3 2 1

Amulet Books are available at special discounts when purchased in quantity for premiums and promotions as well as fundraising or educational use. Special editions can also be created to specification. For details, contact specialsales@abramsbooks.com or the address below.

Amulet Books® is a registered trademark of Harry N. Abrams, Inc.

ABRAMS The Art of Books
195 Broadway, New York, NY 10007
abramsbooks.com

FOR MY
IN-LAWS,
WHO, UNLIKE
ME, ADORE
GARDENING

1

WORD OF THE DAY

EXCAVATOR

A digging machine

Something funny was going on at my school on Monday morning. Not ha-ha funny, but strange and interesting funny.

Baba couldn't drop me off at his regular spot in front of the school. "Why is that truck here?" he asked, frowning. "You better be careful when you walk outside, Marya."

I peered through the window. What I saw made my eyes round like dinner plates: a big yellow truck with a scoop right next door to the school. "Whoa," I whispered. "What is that?"

"That's an excavator," my know-it-all brother, Sal, said.

"Very good, Salman," Baba praised him.

Sal grinned. I guess they teach big words in fifth grade. I stuck out my tongue at him to let him know he didn't impress me.

In third grade, we just called this a truck. Maybe a giant truck. But I loved big words, ever since Mama bought me a Word of the Day diary a few months ago. "What's an ex-ca-va-tor doing here?" I asked.

"No idea," Baba murmured, checking his watch.

"Look, there are more trucks!" Sal said, pointing.

Sure enough, there were two trucks full of dirt on the other side of the street.

"Maybe they found buried treasure in our school," I said excitedly. I'd watched a TV show about buried treasure once. It was full of pirates and sharks, and super exciting!

I made a prayer that there was treasure in Harold Smithers Elementary School. It would make life *way* more interesting. The big chests of coins. The sparkling jewels. It would be totally fabulous!

"Buried treasure isn't real," Sal said, rolling his eyes. "That's only in movies."

"It's real!" I protested. The TV show I watched looked very, very real.

"No, it's not," Sal said firmly.

I scowled, because as usual Sal didn't care about my brilliant idea. Come to think of it, nobody in my family listened to my brilliant ideas. I guess because I was the youngest or whatever.

Sal continued: "Maybe they're going to tear down the school and build an amusement park!"

Sal loved roller coasters. Never mind that he puked when he rode one. He still loved them.

"If they tear down the school, where would we go?" I demanded. It's not that I liked school. I just wanted to have a place to spend time with my best friend, Hanna. And recess in the playground was fun too.

"No school anymore!" Sal cheered.

I rubbed my chin thoughtfully. "Does that mean no homework either?"

"Oh yeah!" Sal and I grinned and gave each other high fives. Then Sal said, "I wish Aliyah could have seen this!"

I rolled my eyes because, first of all, our big sister, Aliyah, was thirteen years old, which meant she thought everything was stupid and boring. Second of all, she got dropped off at the middle school first.

"She'd want the school to turn into a shopping mall!" I snickered.

Sal laughed. "So true!"

"Okay, kids. That's enough!" Baba turned to us.

"The school is open today, so no amusement park or shopping mall."

Sal gave me a secret wink. "That's what they want everyone to think!"

"Time to go to school!" Baba said impatiently. He checked his watch again. "I don't want to be late for work."

Baba worked as a manager in some kind of office. I didn't know what kind, only that they had lots and lots of computers all lined up in rows. Computers were boring, unless you used them to watch your favorite movie or to write an email to your cousins in Pakistan.

I don't think Baba watched movies in his office.

Maybe he wrote emails, but they were probably boring ones.

My emails were the opposite of boring. I always added lots of pictures.

Sal and I scrambled out of the car.

"Be careful!" Baba said as he drove away.

We walked toward the front doors. I went as slowly as possible so I could catch all the action and beeping noises. That's when I realized something: The trucks weren't actually on school property. They were in an empty lot right next to the school.

A few workers stood around, talking to one another. I could see Principal Cleveland waving his arms around. Hmm. This was getting even more interesting. "What do you think's going on?" I asked Sal.

Sal ignored me. As usual.

He waved to his friends and rushed away.

Ugh.

I looked at the trucks some more, then went inside. Hanna was waiting in front of the sports trophy case. That was our usual meeting spot, and she was always on time. I was always late. Always.

Honestly, I tried not to be late, but that's never worked out.

"Hello, Marya!" Hanna said cheerfully. She flipped her long braid. "You're late."

"I was actually on time today," I told her grumpily. "But then I saw all the trucks outside and got distracted."

"You get distracted a lot," she said, smiling.

"It's not my fault," I groaned. "Trucks are my weakness."

"Don't worry," Hanna said. "I was almost late too. My baby sister threw a tantrum at breakfast."

We started walking to class. "Why do you think the trucks are there?" Hanna asked.

I cheered up. "Buried treasure, of course!" I said happily.

"Really?" Hanna's eyes widened. "That sounds awesome!"

"What sounds awesome?" somebody said right next to us. My ears twitched. I didn't even need to turn my head to know who it was. Alexa R., the most annoying person on the planet. Also my next-door neighbor. Also my classmate.

And now also walking right beside me in the school hallway.

I just couldn't get away from her, no matter how much I tried.

"Nothing," I replied, and walked faster. The bell was about to ring, and our teacher, Miss Piccolo, didn't like anyone to be late.

"Buried treasure!" Hanna said. "That would be awesome, right, Alexa?"

I sent Hanna a glare. Why was she always so friendly to my worst enemy? It didn't make any sense.

Alexa sighed. "That's so babyish," she said. "Were you watching one of your silly TV shows, Marya?"

I finally turned and looked at her. She was wearing a fancy dress, and her long blond hair was super shiny. Alexa always looked like she was going to a party. Only one more reason she was so annoying. "It's not silly," I told her. "It could be true. Did you see the truck outside? It's an ex-ca-va-tor. It digs up things."

"Ooh!" Hanna said. "Is that from your Word of the Day book?"

I smiled proudly, because people didn't usually say *ooh* to me. "Sal told me."

Alexa flipped her hair back. "Doesn't mean they're digging up treasure," she insisted. "You're just being silly, Marya Khan."

I opened my mouth to give her a piece of my mind, but the bell rang just then. Alexa pushed me aside like she was the Queen of England. "You're going to be late for class!" she said, and walked away.

I just stood there with my mouth open. "She is so annoying!"

2

WORD OF THE DAY

COMPETITION

A game to win

a prize

anna and I rushed to class, but it was no use. Miss Piccolo was waiting for us at the door. "Hurry up, girls," she called. "No dillydallying."

"What does that even mean?" Hanna whispered in my ear.

"No clue," I replied. Adults said strange things sometimes.

We took our seats. Too bad I was stuck with Alexa. Our seats were in squares of four, and she sat right in front of me. Hanna was next to me, and the fourth seat was empty ever since Tobias moved away.

This was a very unfair situation, because it meant I had to look at Alexa flipping her blond hair all day long. And her party dress.

Today, the dress was orange with black stripes. She looked like a tiger going to a party.

"You're late, Marya," Alexa said. "Just like I knew you would be."

I wrinkled my nose. I knew I'd get in trouble if I shouted. So I just ignored her.

"Are you listening to me, Marya?" she asked, sounding grumpy. I guess the Queen of England didn't like being ignored.

Miss Piccolo passed around math worksheets. "Please stop talking among yourselves!" she warned. "This is rocket math. You have one minute to complete as many questions as you can."

Hanna and I looked at each other. "You'll be first," Hanna whispered.

I grinned because I loved math. Also because I was very good at it.

I went through the problems super quick. They were hard, but multiplication was my jam! And guess what? I finished sixteen problems when Miss Piccolo said, "Time's up!"

I peeked at Hanna's worksheet. Ten problems. "That's okay," I said, patting her hand. Ten was pretty good too.

"You're so fast!" She sighed.

I shrugged. Sometimes I practiced problems on Baba's computer at home, just for fun. That's why I was so fast. Then I peeked at Alexa's worksheet. Sixteen problems, same as me.

Drat.

"I win!" she cried, smiling.

"No, you didn't!" I cried back, only I wasn't smiling even a little bit. "I got the same number as you!"

Miss Piccolo frowned. "Not everything is a competition, students."

Miss Piccolo started to collect the worksheets.

I heard a sound from outside the window that looked onto the playground. Usually I could see the big blue swings. And trees. And lots of birds.

But today, all I saw were trucks. My eyes grew very big. "Why are they digging outside?" I asked Miss Piccolo.

"Good question!" she said. "They're building a community garden next door."

"So, no buried treasure?"

Alexa snorted. I gave her a dirty look.

"No, just some plants and flowers," Miss Piccolo replied cheerfully. "And maybe a gazebo! Won't that be nice!"

"Ooh, there should be a pond too," Alexa said. "Like the park downtown."

I rolled my eyes. "They're not building a pond!"

"How do you know?"

Miss Piccolo clapped her hands to get our attention. "Stop arguing, you two!" she said. "Principal Cleveland will tell us the plan in a special assembly before lunch. You just have to wait until then."

I groaned. "Waiting is the worst."

The bell rang, and we lined up for PE. Hanna told me more about her baby sister. "You're the youngest too, Marya," she whispered. "Just like my sister."

"Being the youngest is awful," I whispered back. "Nobody listens to you. Or thinks you could have great ideas."

"Well, my sister is a toddler. Her best idea is to poop in her diaper and then grin about it."

I wanted to say more about the injustice of being the youngest. Only just then I saw that Alexa got picked as line leader. Again. I could see her orange dress all the way in the front like a neon sign. Talk about injustice.

Before lunch, Principal Cleveland was waiting for us in the cafeteria. The upper grades—that's third, fourth, and fifth—were all lined up in rows. "Good afternoon, students!" Principal Cleveland boomed. "You may have noticed the trucks outside our school."

I looked at him very carefully. What was he going to tell us?

"The city is building a community garden next door," Principal Cleveland explained. "That means it's for everyone!"

The kids cheered. I didn't really care, because I already knew this from Miss Piccolo. I waited to hear more about trucks. Maybe buried treasure. Ooh, or a theme park like Sal said. I wasn't going to be picky at this point.

"The school has asked for a garden to be built here too, in the playground. You students will be allowed to work on it as a special project."

A special project? Gardening? That sounded weird, but also sort of cool. I leaned forward to hear better, only Alexa was blocking my way. "Can you . . . move a little?" I grunted.

She turned and sniffed. "Be nice, Marya. You're taller than me."

Only by a tiny bit, but she acted like I was a giant. "Sorry," I muttered.

Principal Cleveland held up a box. "This is how we'll decide which class gets to go first."

My eyes widened. He was going to pick

someone without looking? What if it turned out to be the kindergarteners? They had zero clue about gardening. Or behaving in general. They were like little puppies that got excited about everything but couldn't really do much without falling over themselves.

"Don't worry," Principal Cleveland said, like he knew what I was thinking. "I'm only going to pick from the upper grades."

I turned to the back of the cafeteria, where Sal stood with the rest of the fifth graders. He was smirking, like he knew they were going to be chosen. I scowled at him. He just smirked some more. Ugh.

Principal Cleveland pulled open the lid of the box and drew out a pink paper.

Hanna grabbed my arm. "I can't look. It's too exciting!" she whispered.

I stared at the pink paper like I could see what was written on it. "I'll look for you, promise."

Hanna dug her fingernails into my arm. Ow! But I forgot all about the pain when Principal Cleveland said: "And the winner is ... Miss Piccolo's third-grade class!"

My mouth dropped open. What? Seriously? Our class cheered and clapped. Miss Piccolo beamed.

"Isn't this amazing?" Hanna squealed, finally letting go of my arm.

I nodded, then turned around to Sal and smirked back at him. He rolled his eyes like it wasn't a big deal, but I could see the fifth graders' faces. They were totally disappointed. Ha! I may not be a big fan of gardens, but being chosen from the whole entire school was pretty amazing.

Principal Cleveland smiled in our direction. "Congratulations, Miss Piccolo! The garden will be ready by the end of the week."

Perfect. I had one week to figure out this gardening business. No big deal.

3

WORD OF THE DAY

LEGENDARY

Well-known

or famous

ama was already in the pickup line when I walked outside that afternoon. I scrunched up my nose when I saw her ancient van because I knew what was going to happen when I got in.

Stink, that's what.

Mama owned a flower shop downtown, so her van was always full of bags of soil (yuck) and fertilizer (gross). Fertilizer was actually animal poop, which was why it stunk so bad.

If you thought a flower shop van would be full of flowers and lovely smells, you'd be sadly mistaken.

A teacher read the card on our windshield and shouted our names. "MARYA KHAN! SALMAN KHAN!"

I quickly got inside the van and took the seat farthest away from all the smelly stuff.

"Where's Salman?" Mama asked.

How was I supposed to know? The fifth graders' line was all the way at the other end of the

dismissal area. Also, Sal never talked to me in school. He thought he was too grown-up for me.

I looked around. A bunch of kids were standing near the fence, staring at the trucks. I saw Sal's black hair. "There he is!" I pointed.

Mama honked her horn. I put my hands over my ears because it sounded like a donkey.

A very loud, sick donkey.

Sal jumped and ran toward the van. "Sorry," he said, panting as he climbed inside.

"I win!" I told him quickly.

"It's not a competition, Marya!" he replied, rolling his eyes.

"You just said that because you lost!" I leaned forward and whispered: "I'm talking about you-know-what."

Basically, I meant the gardening thing. I'd been thinking about it all afternoon. How third graders were chosen to look after it. How we were the best and the coolest. I tried to look sad for my older brother. The loser.

Sal looked totally annoyed. "That was just a lucky draw. It doesn't mean anything."

"Sure!" I patted his head kindly. I didn't care if it was luck. I was finally getting something my older brother wasn't. I may be the youngest in my family, but I got to do something important that he didn't.

If I weren't sitting down in the van, I'd dance a little jig, just to rub it in Sal's face. Only Mama would give me a lecture about seat belts or something, so I just wagged my eyebrows.

Sal scowled.

Mama drove fast, like always. I hung on to the edge of my seat, hoping the bags of soil and/or

poop wouldn't slide in my direction. We stopped at the middle school to pick up Aliyah.

"Guess what!" she said excitedly as she climbed into the front seat. "I'm on the food committee for the eighth-grade spring fair next month!"

"You? Food committee?" I wrinkled my eyebrows.

She turned and shot me a glare, but I was used to it. Aliyah's glares were legendary. "So?" she hissed.

Her hisses were also legendary. Sometimes she reminded me of a wild animal in a zoo, getting mad at everyone who got too close.

I liked teasing her and making her mad. "Well," I said, leaning back in my seat, "you like to eat more than you like to cook."

Sal grinned at me, and I grinned back. No matter how mad we got at each other, we always showed a united front when Aliyah acted up. That was the only way to deal with her grumpiness.

Aliyah was so not amused. "I can cook better than you, Miss burn-the-house-down."

My grin vanished. I'd tried to make a casserole one time and left the oven on too long. It was a big drama, with burnt food and the smoke alarm and lots of angry family members. I crossed my arms over my chest because I didn't want to be reminded. "Hmph!"

Mama patted Aliyah's hand. "It's okay. I'm excited about the food committee. What will you make?"

Aliyah made a face. "I'll have to think about it."

I sat up suddenly because I had a genius idea. "You should make brownies. They're super delicious and everybody loves them. Even grown-ups."

"Don't tell me what to do," Aliyah replied. "I'm the oldest. You're the youngest."

"So what?" I muttered.

Sal said, "Brownies are boring. You should make something cool, like baklava."

"I think that's a great idea!" Mama said as we reached our house. "Good job, Sal!"

Now it was Sal's turn to wag his eyebrows at me, and my turn to scowl. "What about brownies?" I asked, only nobody heard me. They were too busy talking about baklava.

I scowled even more, then stared out the window. Nobody listened to me, ever.

Mama dropped us at home, then went back to her shop. The three of us filed into the house and put our shoes in the hallway closet. "I'm starving!" Sal yelled, and rushed to the kitchen to find some snacks.

"What's new?" I called out after him.

When I reached the kitchen, I saw containers on the counter and the fridge was wide open.

"Leftovers?" Sal asked. He was already digging into a chicken tikka drumstick like he hadn't eaten in years.

I looked at the red spice mix smeared all over his face. Gross.

"No thanks," I replied. I grabbed a packet of peanuts and went into Dadi's room. She was Baba's mom, and my most favorite person in the whole world.

"Salaam, Dadi!" I whispered. It was always a good idea to whisper when you entered her room. If you accidentally woke her from a nap, she got very grumpy.

Good news: Dadi was not napping. She was sitting on her bed, reading a book. "Salaam," she replied, looking up with a warm smile.

I sniffed. Her room always smelled of Vicks, which was my favorite Dadi smell. But today it was mixed with something else. Something much better than Vicks. "What is that?" I asked.

Dadi pointed to a necklace on her nightstand. I looked closer and saw that it was made of white flowers joined together in a circle with thread. "That's jasmine," Dadi said. "The national flower of Pakistan."

I stuck my nose in the flowers and took a deep, deep breath. "Wow." I sighed.

Dadi patted her bed. "Come sit down. Tell me all about school."

I climbed up and sat next to her. "I was the fastest in rocket math again," I reported. "And our class got chosen to make a garden in our school."

"A garden, huh?" Dadi said. "Sounds very nice."

I pointed to her book. "What are you reading?"

She handed it to me. It was in Urdu, which I totally didn't know how to read. But the cover was pretty. It had a chest full of rubies and diamonds. "It's a mystery," she said. "Someone stole all this jewelry from a museum."

I gasped in excitement. "Like buried treasure!"

"Well, it may be buried. Or it may be hidden in a closet." Dadi patted the book. "I don't know yet. That's the mystery."

I ate some peanuts and thought about the treasure in Dadi's book. "Is there a girl detective who's solving the mystery?"

"Don't worry about my book, Marya jaan," Dadi said with a sneaky look. "You can solve a different mystery."

I frowned. "What's that?"

She took the packet from my hand and emptied it into her mouth. "Who ate all the peanuts?"

4

WORD OF THE DAY

BIRYANI

A South Asian

rice dish

That evening, Mama called me to the kitchen before dinner. "I need your help, jaan."

"Why can't Sal and Aliyah help you?" I asked. My good-for-nothing siblings were nowhere to be seen.

"They're coming," Mama said, handing me a stack of plates. "Set the table, please."

"How come I always have to do that?" I moaned.

Aliyah swept into the kitchen. "Cuz you're the youngest!" She grinned and ruffled my head like I was two years old.

"How is this fair?" I demanded. "I'm the youngest, so I have to do all the work?"

Mama shook her head in disappointment. "Do you see me complaining about cooking, jaan? Or cleaning? Or driving you to school . . . ?"

"Okay, okay, I get it!" I said quickly. I really didn't need Mama to start a lecture about all the things she did around the house.

"Good," Mama replied with a smile. "Now set the table, please. We're having biryani."

I felt a lot better at once. Mama's biryani was delicious, and I wanted to gobble it up right this minute. I got plates from a cabinet and arranged them on the table. Then I got spoons from a drawer and placed them next to each plate. I stepped back and tapped a finger on my chin. Something was missing.

"Can I take out the nice glasses?" I asked Mama. Biryani was a special dish, so we needed something special for the table too.

Mama nodded. "Sure."

I opened a cabinet and poked around. There was a box with multicolored glasses inside. We got them from a fancy store in New York City last year. "Perfect," I whispered. I took them out carefully and wiped the insides with a napkin, just in case there was any dust.

"Don't drop them," Aliyah warned.

I totally ignored her.

"Aliyah, hurry up and make the salad," Mama said.

Aliyah frowned. "Ugh, why do I have to do that?"

I giggled under my breath because it was the same thing I'd just said.

Aliyah glared at me. "What are you laughing at?"

"Nothing!"

She took cucumbers and radishes out of the fridge and slammed the door shut. Then she started chopping. I took one look at her face and decided to stay away from her knife. I went to call Dadi. She always took a long time to come to the table.

When Dadi and I got back to the kitchen, Sal and Baba were there, holding grocery bags. "Marya!" Baba exclaimed. "How's my favorite baby girl?"

"Ha!" Sal laughed. "Emphasis on 'baby.'"

I sent him a dirty look. "I'm not a baby!"

Baba came over and kissed me on the top of my head. "You'll always be my baby girl."

Mama smiled at us. "Mine too."

I rolled my eyes very, very hard. I was so over this baby business. I wanted to be a big girl RIGHT THIS MINUTE.

Baba and Sal put the groceries away, talking about football or something. I liked soccer much better, so I didn't say anything. I washed my hands at the sink and then sat down at the table next to Dadi. My plate, spoon, and glass arrangement looked fantastic. Only nobody said anything about it, so I guess they didn't care.

Then I forgot all about it because Mama put a big steaming plate of biryani on the table. I took a deep breath. Yummy.

As usual, the biryani was DELICIOUS. It was also spicy, so I drank a lot of water with it.

Dadi ate without a single drop of water. She was brave.

5

WORD OF THE DAY

FERTILIZER

A product to make

plants grow better

he next morning in class, Miss Piccolo said we should start planning our garden. "Everybody will have a job to do, including the garden leader."

I sat up very straight. A garden leader? That would be the perfect way to prove I was not a baby. So what if nobody at home listened to me? If I became garden leader, everyone in class would have to do exactly as I said.

This was perfect. Sign me up!

Alexa sat up too. She raised her hand importantly. "Who's going to be the leader?" she asked.

Her face was very serious, like she was thinking it was going to be her.

I narrowed my eyes. This wasn't fair. Alexa already got to be line leader every day.

I quickly raised my hand too. "Yes, Miss Piccolo. Who will be in charge?" I gave her my best puppy-dog eyes. They worked so well on Baba.

Miss Piccolo smiled a little, like she knew what I was doing. "I haven't decided yet, Marya."

Seriously? What was she waiting for? How could she start a project without a leader? It didn't make sense. I opened my mouth to ask all my questions, when Miss Piccolo added, "I will let the class know very soon."

Oh. Okay then.

Alexa kept her hand raised. She even waved her fingers around. "I think I should be the leader," she said, "because I have a very big garden at my house."

I groaned. This was even less fair. Alexa lived in a big house with a big garden and a swimming pool. She thought she could get anything she wanted.

She was right most of the time. But not this time. This time, I was going to be the leader. "So what if you have a big garden?" I asked. "You don't do the gardening, do you?"

She rolled her eyes like I was being silly. "Of course not. Our gardener does. But I sit on the deck and watch while he works."

Alexa may be the most annoying person on the planet, but her parents were super busy all the time. Her mom was on the city council—whatever that was—and her dad traveled for business. I wasn't surprised that she spent a lot of time watching her gardener.

Don't tell anyone, but I thought that was really sad.

Still, there was no way I was letting her be leader. "Nobody wears fancy dresses while gardening," I told her.

Alexa flushed. "I'll wear jeans," she promised.

Honestly, I didn't think she owned any jeans. But you never knew. One time she wore denim dungarees and a white straw hat on Halloween. I decided I needed to prove myself to Miss Piccolo. "I should be the leader because my mama owns a flower shop!" I quickly said.

Miss Piccolo got a very excited look on her face. "That's right, Marya! Thank you for reminding me. Maybe your mom can help teach us about gardening."

I blinked at her. I'd just said that to show I knew more about plants than Alexa. I really didn't want Mama to be helping out at school. That would be weird. "She's got a *flower* shop," I said. "Not a garden shop."

Miss Piccolo waved her hand. "Doesn't matter. I'm sure she will be happy to help."

She wasn't wrong. Mama was always helping

everyone. She was a totally nice and kind person, and the best mama in the world.

"Off topic!" Alexa interrupted.

Oh yeah, the garden leader business. I took a deep breath. "Anyway, I know more about plants. And flowers. And fertilizer." I looked at the class firmly, like I knew exactly what I was talking about.

"What's that?" Alexa asked, wrinkling her nose.

"That's poop," I explained. "Only it's the good kind that plants need to grow big and strong."

The whole class burst into laughter.

"Ew!" Alexa shouted. "Marya Khan, you're disgusting!"

"Garden stuff is pretty disgusting," I agreed. "You shouldn't be the leader if you can't take it."

"Quiet, please!" Miss Piccolo called out. "I'll decide later." She handed out big blank papers. "Let's start planning out the perfect garden."

I took a paper and stared at it. "What's there to plan?" I asked. "Just put in some dirt, then the flowers. Then water them. Simple!"

"Don't forget the poop!" Antonio laughed.

"Fertilizer," I said patiently. "That's more polite."

"Planning a garden is important," Miss Piccolo explained. "You want to decide how it will look, which plants will be used, and where everything will go. You can't just put things willy-nilly."

Hanna and I exchanged a look. Miss Piccolo really had a strange way of talking.

"How would we decide?" Hanna asked.

"Ooh! I know!" Alexa cried. "My gardener says some plants need sunlight, and some need shade. If you put a plant in the wrong place, it could die."

I rolled my eyes because I thought she was being totally dramatic.

Then Miss Piccolo smiled proudly like Alexa was brilliant. Ugh. Why didn't I think of sunlight and shade?

Miss Piccolo switched on the smartboard. "Let's look at some pictures of gardens."

She turned away, which meant Alexa and I could look at each other without anyone noticing. "I'll be the leader, you'll see," Alexa said sweetly.

"Sure, dream on." I crossed my arms over my chest and gave her my best mean-face. That's what I called it when someone scrunched their eyes and scowled like an angry lion.

Alexa quickly turned back to the smartboard. That meant my mean-face had worked. Perfect.

When I got home, I collapsed on the couch with a great big sigh. I had to think of a way to be garden leader. A way to let Miss Piccolo know I was perfect for the job.

"Stop being so dramatic, Marya," Aliyah said, smirking.

I gave her a dirty look. "You're not the only one with drama in her life, you know!"

She rolled her eyes. "Yeah, right."

I sat up. Just because Aliyah was thirteen, she thought she knew everything. "You don't know anything about gardens or trucks or line leaders!" I sputtered.

She sat down next to me. "What gardens?"

She wasn't hissing or saying mean things, so I decided to tell her the whole story. "Alexa wants to be in charge," I finished. "But that's going to be me. I'll do anything to be in charge."

"Being in charge isn't all it's cracked up to be," she told me.

I gasped. Who was Aliyah kidding? Being in charge was the best. You could decide what to do and order people around and give punishments. It was awesome!

Aliyah continued: "I'm in charge of the food committee, but I can't figure out what to make."

"Just make brownies." I shrugged. I totally didn't understand her problem.

She shook her head. "You don't know middle-school kids. They like cool things."

I thought brownies were the coolest thing on earth. Well, that and pizza. But maybe middle-school kids forgot important stuff like that when they became teenagers. Who knew? Aliyah had definitely forgotten her manners when she turned thirteen.

"I need to make the best food ever!" Aliyah sighed a big sigh, just like me.

I blinked. That was it! That's how I'd be the garden leader instead of Alexa! I'd plan the best garden and ask Mama for the best help, and then

Miss Piccolo would have to choose me. Because I'd be the best. Better than Alexa or anyone else.

I jumped up. I couldn't wait to put Operation Be a Leader into action.

Soon, I'd have the most fabulous garden in Harold Smithers Elementary!

6

WORD OF THE DAY

GLUM

Thinking sad

thoughts

I told Hanna all about Operation Be a Leader near the trophy case the next morning.

"What do you know about being a leader?" she asked, frowning. "You're the youngest in your family. You're basically a follower."

Hmm. She wasn't wrong about the youngest part. I thought for a minute, then I got an excellent idea. "You're the oldest," I said to Hanna, grabbing her arm. "You can teach me!"

Hanna raised her eyebrows. "My baby sister is two years old. She just wants to follow me around."

"That's perfect!" I told her. "I also want people to follow me around and do what I say."

"She never does what I say," Hanna protested. "Even though I'm her big sister."

I waved like it was no big deal. "So what makes you a good big sister?"

Hanna shrugged. "Basically, knowing what to do and what not to do."

I grabbed her arm again. "So, step number one: Show that you have knowledge!"

"Ow!" Hanna pulled her arm away. "Yes, you could say that."

The bell rang, but I hardly noticed. I was too busy thinking. I remembered how everyone in the class had looked at me when I'd told them about soil and fertilizer. That was me showing them I knew stuff. Important garden stuff.

All I had to do was keep doing that over and over. Then everyone, including Alexa, would realize I was born to be the leader.

I got my first chance at recess. Miss Piccolo made us stay inside because the playground was closed off. Normally, this would make me very sad because recess was my favorite time of the day.

But today I didn't mind. There was a man in the playground digging up a big rectangle behind the swings. We all watched from the classroom window as he took piles of dirt and threw them away like they were as light as air.

"He's strong," Antonio muttered.

"What's he doing?" Hanna asked.

Ooh, I knew this! "He's making our garden!" I said loud enough for Miss Piccolo to hear.

Miss Piccolo looked very pleased. "That's right, Marya. He's part of the team working next door. Principal Cleveland asked him to come today. This way, we can get started on planting soon!"

"Cool," Omar said, grinning at me. He was a quiet kid, but he always had something nice to say.

I grinned back. "Does that mean I can be the leader?" I asked Miss Piccolo.

She patted my head. "No."

Drat. I stopped myself from stomping my foot. Operation Be a Leader was going to be more difficult that I'd thought.

Miss Piccolo started talking about gardens. You'd think that would be super boring, but surprisingly it was not. "A garden has many purposes," she told us. "You need to decide if you want a vegetable garden or something with pretty flowers."

"Why can't we have both?" Hanna asked.

"You could," Miss Piccolo replied. "But you have limited space, and you don't want it to look like a hodgepodge."

I rolled my eyes. Miss Piccolo was basically the strangest Word of the Day person I'd ever met.

Thankfully, she didn't notice. She went on and on about different types of gardens and even something called a wild garden, which sounded pretty amazing. Only then you wouldn't really need a garden leader, so I was going to act like it wasn't even an option. Our school garden definitely needed a leader.

And that leader was going to be me.

By the end of the day, the man had finished making the garden bed for us. It was higher than the rest of the ground and had wooden sides. The man had also put in a sprinkler to water our plants.

"It's so nice!" Hanna sighed as we packed up our things.

"My backyard at home is way better," Alexa told her.

I totally believed that, because Alexa's house and yard were humungous.

"The garden is almost ready for you, class!" Miss Piccolo told us just before dismissal. "Please work on your garden plans tonight. I'll pick the best one tomorrow morning."

I perked up. The best was going to be me, I just knew it!

Then my shoulders slumped. What was I thinking? I knew nothing about garden plans. Or being in charge. If only someone would help me.

When I got home, Baba was in the kitchen,

checking his phone. I remembered it was his work-from-home day. "Salaam, Baba," I said in a grumpy voice.

He leaned down to kiss my head. "Why so glum, my love?" he asked.

"I'm hungry," I told him, stomping off to the pantry to find something to eat.

"I can make you a grilled cheese sandwich," he offered. I sat at the counter and watched him. Baba cooked grilled cheese in the best way: all gooey cheese and browned bread.

"Anything interesting happened at school?" Baba asked.

"I need to come up with a fabulous plan for our school garden," I replied.

"Fabulous, eh?" He pointed to the sandwich. "Like that?"

I giggled and took a bite. "Yes, that's definitely fabulous."

Baba picked up his phone. "You know, when I was a kid, I visited a fabulous place once. It's called Shalimar Gardens, in Pakistan."

My ears perked up. "Really?"

He searched for it on his phone and showed me a picture. My eyes grew big. The Shalimar Gardens were definitely fabulous. The plants were in rectangular beds, and there was a rectangular pond in the center. "Wow!" I whispered.

"Nice, isn't it?" Baba replied, smiling.

"More like amazing!"

Baba put his phone away and left. I ate the rest of my sandwich quietly. Then I went back to my room and found the paper Miss Piccolo had given

us. It was time to draw the plan. I closed my eyes and imagined my garden, the one where I was in charge and everything was exactly like I said. Green grass. Tall trees. A rectangular pond in the center. I took out my coloring pencils and drew it out just like I imagined it.

On top, I wrote MARYA'S FABULOUS GARDEN.

All I needed now were flowers. I couldn't decide which one was my favorite. I liked roses for their smell. But sunflowers were super pretty. Oh, and Hanna's favorite were violets, with their purple petals.

I couldn't decide, so I drew them all. Red for the roses, yellow for the sunflowers, and purple for the violets. Then I labeled them so there was no mistake.

At the last minute, I remembered Dadi's special flower: jasmine. The national flower of Pakistan. I added that too. It would make my fabulous garden even more awesome.

I grinned when I was finished. Miss Piccolo was sure to love this plan.

7

WORD OF THE DAY

ANALYZE

To think about

something carefully

The next day, we stayed inside for recess again. Everyone groaned because that was completely not fair. "The man is gone now," Hanna pointed out.

"Yes, but some of his equipment is still lying around," Miss Piccolo said. "You could get hurt with it."

"But it's recess!" Antonio protested.

"I realize that, young man." Miss Piccolo patted her desk. "Students, if you've finished your garden plans, please place them here. If you still need some time, you can take the rest of this period."

I started to look through my backpack, but I did it super slowly. I wanted to wait to hand my plan over so I could put it on top of the pile. That way, our teacher could see it first.

Miss Piccolo sat down and started reading from a big folder. A few kids got up and put their papers on the desk. Miss Piccolo didn't even look up.

I decided I needed to hand my garden plan

directly to her. I wanted her to actually examine it. Inspect it. Analyze it.

Antonio jumped up and down. "I'm bored! What should we do?"

Miss Piccolo looked up and sighed. "You can do whatever you want inside the classroom," she said, "as long as you don't go overboard."

"What's that mean?" Alexa asked.

I remembered Operation Be a Leader, and how I was supposed to have all the knowledge. "It means don't do too much," I told her.

"I never do too much," she replied.

Antonio laughed. "I thought it meant jumping off a ship into the water!"

I imagined our entire class on a ship. Of course, I'd be the captain, only Alexa would probably be fighting me for that too. Maybe she could be the evil pirate I'd have to defeat.

If evil pirates wore party dresses, that is.

Miss Piccolo sighed loudly. She got up and started a movie on the smartboard. Some of the

kids settled down to watch. Others stood at the window and looked outside. Antonio and one of his friends kept doing jumping jacks, but they were quiet. I guess that was the opposite of going overboard.

I looked around. This was the perfect time to show Miss Piccolo my plan. She looked up when I reached her desk. "What is it, Marya?" she asked, looking suspicious.

I'm not sure why she was suspicious. I was always such a good girl. Seriously.

I put my drawing on her desk and smoothed it out. "Ta-da!" I smiled some more.

Miss Piccolo peered at my drawing. "What is this?" she asked.

I tried very hard not to roll my eyes. It was obvious what it was, on account of the big heading that said MARYA'S FABULOUS GARDEN.

I pointed to it. "It's my garden plan," I told her. "Like you asked."

She picked up the paper and examined it carefully. "This is very good."

Alexa came up behind me and slapped another paper on the desk. It was bigger than mine and had more flowers on it. Plus, it had a pretty border like a wedding invitation we'd once gotten in the mail. I leaned over to read the heading: ALEXA'S AMAZING GARDEN.

"Did you cheat from me?" I gasped.

Alexa gave me a shocked look. "What? I made this at home last night. Marya, you're being very silly right now."

I wasn't, but I zipped my mouth shut. Not really, just in my mind. I even locked it and threw away the key. I had a feeling Miss Piccolo didn't want us being too loud or hyper.

Miss Piccolo studied Alexa's drawing too. Then she put down our papers. "Both of these are good. I need to look at everyone's papers before I decide who the leader will be."

Now I was the one being suspicious. "But you told us . . ."

She pointed to our seats. "Go sit down and watch the movie, please."

Alexa and I looked at each other and said "Ugh" at the exact same time.

During last period, Miss Piccolo clapped her hands for silence. "I have an announcement, children!" she called out.

I sat up straight. This was it, I knew it. The leader announcement.

My heart pounded in my chest like a drum. I looked over at Alexa. She was also sitting up very straight.

I gave her a little smile, just to tell her not to freak out when I won. She reached over and squeezed my hand. It felt good, because right now giant butterflies were flying around in my stomach.

Okay, maybe sometimes we were friends. Not a big deal.

"Everyone's garden plans were very good,"

Miss Piccolo continued. "But the best ones were made by Alexa Rhodes and Marya Khan."

Hanna squealed beside me. I grinned at her. I could see where this was going. Victory was going to be so sweet!

"So who is the winner?" Omar called out.

I waited to hear my name, only it never came. "Nobody," Miss Piccolo replied.

"Nobody?" I asked faintly. How was that possible?

Miss Piccolo winked at me. "I'm making both girls garden leaders."

What? I let go of Alexa's hand like it had burned me. "You can't—" I began.

"She can," Hanna pointed out helpfully, whispering in my ear. "She's the teacher."

"I know!" I whispered back angrily. It wasn't fair. I couldn't be the leader in my family because I was the youngest. Now I couldn't be the leader in class either, even though we were all the same age.

Alexa bounced in her seat. "Thank you, Miss Piccolo! What a great honor!"

"But . . ." I started. Only I didn't really know what to say next, so I stopped.

"Don't look so upset, Marya," Miss Piccolo said. "It will be good for you girls to work together for once."

She went on to explain that the garden would be ready for us bright and early on Monday morning. I guess that was good. I had some time to figure out how to share being a leader with my biggest enemy in the whole wide world.

After the awful announcement, Alexa turned to me and squealed. "This will be so much fun, Marya!"

I crossed my arms over my chest and gave her my most ferocious scowl. "No, it won't."

She just smiled. "You'll see. It will be awesome!"

8

WORD OF THE DAY

RESPONSIBILITY

A job or duty

The next day was Friday. Hanna was absent, which meant Alexa and I sat at our square table all alone.

"Look what I made, Marya," Alexa said, pointing to her chest. She was wearing a purple dress, and on her chest was a name tag. It said ALEXA, CO-CAPTAIN.

I stared at it. Where did she even get that? And who said we were captains? "Gardening is not a sport," I told her.

She waved her hand like a queen. "It doesn't matter." She took out another name tag from her backpack and handed it to me. "Here's yours."

MARYA, CO-CAPTAIN. What nonsense. I put it on very, very slowly. "It looks weird," I muttered.

Omar leaned toward our table. "That looks great!" he whispered. "I'm glad you two are the captains!"

I gave up and smiled because who was I kidding? Co-*captain* sounded even better than *leader*.

Alexa clapped her hands in delight. "Perfect! We look like twins."

Miss Piccolo took attendance. Then she handed our garden plans back to us. I took mine and put it into my backpack. I didn't care if Alexa and I were co-leaders or co-captains or whatever. My plan was the best one.

"Let's make sure we're all ready for our garden project on Monday!" Miss Piccolo said.

Alexa raised her arm very high. "Ooh, Miss! Marya and I got our name tags, see?"

"Yup," I added. "We're ready for Monday."

Miss Piccolo raised her eyebrows. "You think

having a name tag makes you ready to be a leader, Marya?"

I frowned, because what else did we need? I'd won the leader position. Okay, I had to share it with the most annoying girl on the planet, but I was ignoring that part. This was going to be a piece of cake. That garden was going to be fabulous, just like my plan.

Shaking her head, Miss Piccolo wrote *Leader Responsibilities* on the board. Then she added:

"This sounds complicated," I protested. I wasn't even sure this list was correct. Being a leader was more about giving orders, like everyone in my house did.

Alexa patted my hand. "My gardener says learning about plants is the most important thing. You don't want to make mistakes."

"What kind of mistakes?" Omar asked.

Alexa chewed her lip. "I'm not really sure," she replied. "He's really good at his job, so he doesn't really make any mistakes."

"Maybe you should ask him," I said jokingly. It was still strange to me that the Rhodes family had a gardener. In my family, it was Dadi who watered all the plants in our backyard. There weren't many, and sometimes I helped her.

Alexa smiled at me. "Good idea," she said. "I'll get back to you next week, Co-captain!"

Ugh.

"Attention, students!" Miss Piccolo exclaimed. Then she started talking about how plants needed sunlight to make food.

I stood alone at dismissal, missing Hanna very much. Everyone was talking and laughing. I fiddled with my name tag, looking around.

When Mama arrived, the most terrible thing happened. The teacher calling out names shouted: "MARYA KHAN! SALMAN KHAN!" Then I almost fainted because she screamed, "ALEXA RHODES!" right afterward.

Wait, what was happening? Alexa's big blue car wasn't anywhere in the line.

I was one hundred percent sure it was a mistake, until Queen Alexa came running up to my

stinky van and slid inside right after me. "What . . .
what . . . ?" I sputtered.

Mama looked at us in the mirror. "Your teacher
called me," she explained. "Said you girls were
building a garden and needed my help."

"We don't need—" I started.

"That's wonderful, Mrs. Khan," Alexa interrupted. Then she kicked me in the shin just so I'd
get the message.

"Ow!" I whispered. But she was right. I was
being rude. I smiled at Mama in the mirror. "Yup,
wonderful."

Sal scrambled in with a grin. "Hey, are we having a party?"

I groaned. "Like we'd ever invite you to our
party!"

Alexa giggled in her signature annoying way.
"It's sort of like a party," she said. "In a van."

Mama started driving. "We're going to my shop
to pick out flowers for your school garden," Mama
explained. "Alexa's mom gave me permission."

I was too busy sputtering to reply.

Alexa was too busy looking around the van to reply. I waited for her to say something mean or rude, Alexa-style.

Then I realized the van was empty. No bags of poop fertilizer. No potting soil. And no stink.

In fact, it smelled kind of nice. Like that air freshener Baba had in his car that smelled like trees.

Mama looked at me in the mirror again. "I cleaned it up," she said, winking at me.

My shoulders slumped. Phew. That was close. There was no way I wanted any of my classmates to enter this van and find smelly things all over. Not even Alexa.

"This is a really nice van," Alexa said politely to Mama.

"Why, thank you, Alexa dear!" Mama smiled as she drove.

I rolled my eyes. Alexa knew how to suck up to grown-ups, that was for sure.

After dropping Sal and Aliyah at home, Mama

took us to her shop. Alexa's mouth dropped open. "Wow, this is awesome, Mrs. Khan!" she gushed.

"Why, thank you, Alexa dear," Mama said again.

I rolled my eyes again. If this went on, my eyes would get stuck in my head or something. "It's just a flower shop, Alexa," I muttered.

Mama showed us the flowers. There were roses and sunflowers and violets, all the ones I really liked. They were in little brown flowerpots, lined up in rows on the counter. "My favorites!" Alexa squealed.

I frowned. How were they her favorites? They were mine! I snatched my garden drawing out of my backpack. Alexa took hers out too, only more carefully. We compared them. Her plan was totally different. It had straight rows, and no pond like the Shalimar Gardens.

But one thing was the same: the flowers. Roses. Sunflowers. Violets. She'd even labeled them, just like me.

"Oh, that's adorable," Mama said, smiling. "Both of you chose the same flowers!"

Alexa smiled back. "That's because we're friends, Mrs. Khan."

I wanted to stomp my foot and scream. Alexa R. definitely wasn't my friend. But Mama was giving me a warning look, like she was saying, *Behave, missy!*, so I just muttered, "Yeah, right."

Alexa smiled bigger and put her arm around me. "Best friends!" she said, giggling.

Okay, no need to go overboard.

I turned away and saw a bird feeder in the corner. It was in the shape of a house, with a red roof and round circles where birds could enter. I grabbed it quickly. I had to have something different from annoying Alexa. We couldn't be the same—it just wasn't possible. "I want this too!" I told Mama stubbornly.

Alexa giggled some more.

9

WORD OF THE DAY

EMBARRASSMENT

Something

that makes you

uncomfortable

On Monday morning, Mama parked her van in the school parking lot. "Ready, jaan?" she asked. She was dressed in her favorite green outfit, with the white hijab.

I scrambled out and stood on the sidewalk. "Ready."

Mama opened the back doors of the van and took out a big rolling cart. She started loading it with the flowerpots I'd seen in her shop on Friday. I

counted them carefully. Six roses. Six sunflowers. Six violets. Plus, four plants with tiny strawberries hanging from them. They were ADORABLE!

Then I realized something was missing. Something super important. "Where's the jasmine?" I asked, my heart sinking.

Mama frowned. "Jasmine flowers are really expensive, Marya. And I didn't have them in the shop anyway. I'd have to special-order them."

"But . . . those *are* really special." I could hear myself whining, but I couldn't help it. If I was going to be leader, I had to give orders. Stay in command.

Mama gave me a stern look. Okay, I guess leaders couldn't really command their moms. Which was totally unfair. I bet Alexa's mom listened to everything she said.

"No jasmine, Marya," Mama told me firmly. "Now help me load these pots and take them inside."

I sighed very loudly so she'd know I wasn't happy. She didn't budge, so I helped her load all the flowerpots onto the cart. I saw my bird feeder sitting in the corner of the van, and I put it onto the cart too. "I'm not sure that's a good idea," Mama protested. "You don't want too many birds flocking into your garden, do you?"

"Birds are great," I replied. "Cute and feathery and . . . and . . . with beautiful singing voices."

Mama laughed. "Okay, if you say so."

She began to push the cart toward the school. I closed the van's doors and followed her. There were lots of kids in the hallway. Everyone turned to look at us. "Great flowers!" someone called out.

I scowled. You know what would've been really great? Jasmine.

When we reached my classroom, Mama said, "I have to talk with your principal. I'll be back soon." She waved and walked away with her cart.

"Good luck!" I called. Talking to Principal Cleveland was in my top five worst things to do in life. Also on that list were getting eaten by a shark and falling in stinky garbage.

During recess, Miss Piccolo took us to the playground. Mama had already unloaded her cart and set everything on the ground. She sat on a bench near the swings, hands folded on her lap. "Ready to get started?" she asked cheerfully.

The kids gathered around Mama like she was their favorite teacher. Alexa was wearing jeans today, just like she'd said she would. They were light blue, with a heart on each knee.

Even Alexa's jeans were fancy.

"Ready!" Antonio shouted.

"That's Marya's mom!" Alexa told everyone loudly.

I groaned, because having your mom in school as a teacher was so embarrassing.

Mama smiled at me, then at the whole class. "Yes, that's right. But Marya will receive no special treatment from me. No need to worry."

I groaned again, because it would be nice to get some special treatment in the form of jasmine flowers.

Mama smoothed her hijab and began: "I'm going to teach you the basics of gardening."

"I already know—" Alexa began.

I elbowed her in the side. How dare she interrupt my mama? "Shush!"

Like an expert, Mama taught the class how to plant the flowers into the ground. It was easy: Dig a small hole. Take the flower out of its pot. Place it carefully into the ground. Finally, cover the roots with the soil again. Repeat until the flowers were done.

Six roses. Six sunflowers. Six violets. That

was six times three. Eighteen flowers. Plus, the four strawberry plants. That made twenty-two. I figured that out faster in my head than a rocket math assignment.

"Marya and Alexa, step forward, please!" Miss Piccolo said.

I perked up. Since Alexa and I were leaders now, we got to be in charge. I guess that was okay for now. Only being the leader meant more than ordering everyone around, apparently. According to Mama, I had to help the kids in my class whenever they made a mistake.

Which happened all the time.

Omar dug a giant hole for his flower. It was big enough to plant a tree. I had to help him make the hole smaller by filling it back in with dirt.

Antonio almost smashed a pot on the ground. Alexa grabbed it just in time.

"Whoa!" she whispered.

"Sorry," said Antonio.

Alexa and I flashed smiles at each other. Then I remembered we were supposed to be enemies, and I looked away.

Too bad Mama noticed our *moment*. "Our co-leaders are really working hard!" Mama told Miss Piccolo, wiggling her eyebrows.

I rolled my eyes at that. Hmph! Co-leaders. Seriously, who thought this was a good idea?

Just then, I saw Hanna smashing dirt with her hands. "Slowly," I said. "The roots are delicate."

She grinned at me.

I grinned too, because maybe—just maybe—being co-leader wasn't so bad.

Then Alexa spoiled it. When all the flowers were planted, Miss Piccolo stood with her finger on her chin. "I think something is missing . . ."

Alexa came over with her backpack. "I know, Miss Piccolo!" She opened the bag and took out a little red gnome. "Ta-da!"

The whole class went "Ooh!" like it was a diamond tiara or something. I scowled. What good was a gnome, I'd like to know!

Miss Piccolo took the gnome and placed it in the corner of our garden patch. "There! He can watch over our plants."

The class cheered.

I crossed my arms over my chest. First, I had to give up my dream of a jasmine garden. Then I was forced to share leader duties with my worst enemy. And now I had to look at this gnome every day?

I stomped over to Mama's rolling cart and grabbed my bird feeder. "I want to put this up!" I said loudly.

The kids cheered again, which made me less mad. Mama took the bird feeder from my hand and strung it up on a tree branch.

The bell rang, and everyone started to leave. I stood near the tree, looking at my bird feeder.

"That's not a good idea, you know," Alexa whispered.

"It's more useful than a gnome," I muttered. What did she have against birds anyway?

"The birds will come and eat our plants," she insisted.

I shook my head. We got birds in our backyard all the time. Dadi scattered old bread and sunflower seeds on the patio for them to eat. They never bothered our plants. "You worry too much, Alexa. Birds are awesome. You'll see."

10

WORD OF THE DAY

CREATIVE

Using your

imagination

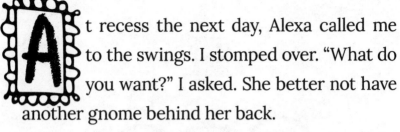

At recess the next day, Alexa called me to the swings. I stomped over. "What do you want?" I asked. She better not have another gnome behind her back.

She smiled excitedly and waved a paper in my face. "Look what I made!" she exclaimed.

I took the paper from her. It was a chores list. Cleaning the flower beds. Watering the plants. Removing dead leaves. Ew, gross. There was also something about insect control. Double gross.

"We should spend a few minutes every recess working on these chores," Alexa said. "If we all work together, we'll get things done quickly and still have time to play."

"We?" I exclaimed. "As in the co-captains too?" I shook my head firmly. She could do the chores with the others. I was the one who'd be giving orders. Maybe it was time I became Queen Marya.

"Yup!" Alexa nodded just as firmly.

"But we're the leaders," I sputtered, thinking of the chores at my house. There's no way I needed them in school too.

Alexa frowned at me like I was being very silly. "Everyone will have a job, Marya. That's only fair. We can't expect the others to do their chores if we don't."

Ugh, why did she have to make so much sense? Still, the idea of giving everyone a job wasn't bad. She was right: If everyone got their jobs done quickly, we'd still have time to play at recess. I ran to the classroom and came back with a pack of index cards and my pencil box. I sat on a bench and started making a card for each student.

"Good idea," Alexa praised me.

"Thanks," I mumbled.

She watched me for a few minutes, then sat beside me and picked up a card. "I can help."

I shrugged. Don't tell anyone, but working with Alexa was fun. We got it done super fast, and I used my coloring pencils to make a little picture on each card. A leaf. A flower. Even a little scarecrow.

"You're very creative, Marya," Alexa said.

"Er, thanks?"

When we finished, Alexa stood up and clapped her hands. "Please gather around!" she shouted, just like Principal Cleveland.

I was in charge of handing out the index cards. Hanna inspected hers like she was studying for

a test. "I didn't know gardening would be hard work," she said.

I patted her shoulder because I totally agreed with her. Then I reminded myself about Operation Be a Leader. "It'll be fun!" I told her. "Just follow my orders and you'll be fine."

"And mine too," Alexa added.

Miss Piccolo frowned at us. "Being a leader is more than just bossing everyone around, girls."

"We know!" Alexa and I both said together. But in my mind, I was saying the opposite.

"Cool," Antonio said, then stuffed his index card into his pocket without even looking at it.

I glared at him. "You better not forget to do your chore!"

He shrugged and ran off to play tag with his friends. "See ya later!"

I stomped my foot. This wasn't going exactly the way I'd hoped. "Everybody needs to do their chores!" I called out.

Okay, I may have shouted. I tried to calm my voice down. "Please start working!"

Nobody turned around. They kept doing what-ever they were doing. Playing. Talking. Running around laughing.

Alexa pulled me toward the garden. "Come on, let's get started. They'll come when they see us working."

I doubted that would happen, but I followed her anyway. Miss Piccolo was watching us, her arms crossed over her chest.

I looked at the chores list. Alexa and I both had cleaning duty. We chose opposite ends of the garden and started picking up litter. There was trash all around the flowers, small things like a plastic water bottle cap and scraps of paper. The big tree at the edge, where my bird feeder was hanging, was shedding leaves. Alexa and I gathered all the trash in a pile.

"This is awful," I whispered to Alexa. "The index cards totally failed."

"It's okay," she whispered back. "At least we're together."

Only now we had no time to play at recess. I kept looking around, but none of our classmates came to help. Even Hanna wasn't there. Okay, she fell down in the mud and Miss Piccolo sent her to the nurse for a bandage. "I'll help tomorrow, I promise!" she'd said as she went inside.

By the time the bell rang, all the chores were done. By Alexa and me.

Also, guess what? I wasn't happy about it. In fact, I was the opposite of happy. I was sweaty and mad.

Operation Be a Leader was officially terrible.

11

WORD OF THE DAY

CATASTROPHE

An event causing

great damage

have a plan!" I announced to Alexa on Wednesday.

I'd thought all night about how to fix Operation Be a Leader before it went bust. Finally, I came up with a super-duper brilliant idea to convince our classmates to do their chores: brownies.

Everybody loved brownies. Most people would do anything for a delicious gooey square of brownie, especially if they were hungry.

All I had to do was promise brownies to whoever

did their chores. Then I'd sit back and watch the work get done under my leadership eye.

The only problem with that plan? I still needed to convince Aliyah to make brownies for her spring fair. And if she agreed, she could easily make some for me too. That would be harder, since she was a meanie. I decided I'd think about that later.

Being a leader was all about having a good plan.

The bell rang, and Alexa whispered, "Tell me later," like we were besties or something.

Miss Piccolo called us to our seats. "Rocket math time, students!"

We sat down and got to work. I was imagining delicious brownies, but I still finished seventeen problems in one minute, which meant I was basically a genius. Then I saw Alexa got the same number of answers, which made me growl. Why did she have to be the same as me at everything? Why couldn't I beat her at anything? It was unbelievable.

"Look!" Hanna said, pointing to the window. "A blue jay!"

Sure enough, there was a blue bird sitting on my bird feeder. Wait, not just one. I counted three blue jays and one pigeon. There were also several little brown birds with tiny beaks. It looked like a birdie party.

"Aren't they pretty?" Hanna asked, her eyes wide.

For about five seconds, I was happy to see birds on my bird feeder. Then I realized they weren't eating birdseed. They were flying over the plants in our garden. One of the blue jays even pecked at a strawberry plant.

Come to think of it, the strawberry plant looked like a boring old bush with only one strawberry. What was happening right now?

"You're turning red, Marya," Alexa said. "Are you feeling sick?"

"I'm fine!" I whispered.

Actually, I may have shouted, because Miss Piccolo looked at me with a big frown on her face. "Use your indoor voice, please," she said.

I jumped up and ran to the window. "Hey!" I yelled, tapping on the glass. "Shoo! Fly away, birdie."

"Marya Khan!" Miss Piccolo gasped. "Do you want to visit the principal's office?"

"No," I replied, hanging my head. "But the birds—"

Miss Piccolo got up and pulled the blind over the window. "Go back to your seat, please," she said very sternly.

"What happened?" Alexa whispered.

I didn't say anything. I couldn't. I kept thinking about my bird feeder and how she'd told me it wasn't a good idea. How it would make birds come into the garden.

News flash: Alexa had been right, and I'd been wrong.

When the bell for recess finally rang, I ran outside so fast, Miss Piccolo couldn't stop me. Alexa was right behind me. I couldn't wait to see our garden in all its fabulousness. That would cheer me up.

Only when we got there, everything was horrible.

The strawberries were gone. The flowers were wilted. The bird feeder was totally empty.

Plus, there was all sorts of trash in the flower beds. Pieces of paper and candy wrappers. Also, three entire plastic water bottles. The garden was not fabulous at all.

It was a catastrophe.

"Oh no!" Miss Piccolo whispered. "I wonder what happened."

I felt like screaming, because I knew exactly what had happened. Kindergarten had their

recess in first period, and they were messy. Even worse, bird thieves destroyed our garden and ate all our strawberries. Alexa looked at the mess, then at my bird feeder. Then she turned to stare at me. I waited for her to say, *I told you* so.

Only guess what? She didn't say anything. She just clapped her hands and shouted, "Okay, everyone, let's clean this up!"

Everyone ran to do their chores. Even Miss Piccolo helped. My mouth fell open. The kids in our class followed Alexa without question. She didn't have to bribe anyone with brownies. And she never got mad, even when my bird feeder brought thieves into our garden.

It was official. I wasn't a good leader. Alexa was.

I didn't speak to anyone when I got home. I just curled up on my bed and drew jasmine flowers all over my sketchbook. Over and over, page after page.

It was silly, but it helped me feel better. When Mama called me to set the table for dinner, I didn't complain even a little bit. I'd learned my lesson the hard way. If people didn't do their chores, everything was a catastrophe. A big, messy, trashy catastrophe.

At dinner, Aliyah went on and on about the stupid spring fair, but I didn't even look up. Finally, she sighed heavily and said, "I guess I'll just make brownies."

I perked up. "Really?"

"You have to help me," Aliyah warned. "Since it was your idea."

I nodded quickly. I would never complain about helping in the house again.

Except when I had to clean the bathroom. I'd definitely complain a lot then.

The next day, Alexa asked me, "Are you okay?" in first period. I just nodded and kept my eyes on Miss Piccolo.

"Don't worry, we'll fix it," she whispered to me.

I wasn't sure what she meant, but I didn't ask.

Then I got the biggest surprise. Mama showed up at recess with her rolling cart. It had all sorts of gardening supplies piled up on it. The entire class gathered around her.

"Miss Piccolo told me what happened," Mama said. "No need to feel bad. This is part of the learning experience."

"What?" I frowned. "Getting our garden destroyed is part of the experience?"

I was so upset at this, I forgot that I said *our* garden instead of *my* garden. Alexa gave me a happy smile, which I totally ignored.

"Yes, absolutely," Miss Piccolo said, coming up to us and clapping her hands for attention. "Anyone want to share what they learned?"

Hanna raised her hand. "That birds are thieves?"

Everyone laughed. I scowled because it was true.

"Well, yes." Miss Piccolo laughed. "But more important, that you have to protect your plants from birds and insects."

"And worms," Antonio added, laughing.

"Ew!" the class groaned.

"Worms are good for the soil," I told him. I knew this from all the times Mama talked about her flower shop. It was second to my knowledge about poop fertilizer.

"That's right, Marya," Mama said, smiling proudly. "What else did you kids learn?"

Alexa raised her hand. "Don't wear dresses while gardening?"

Everyone laughed again. Alexa's jeans today had actual gemstones on the bottom hems. They glittered in a line around her ankles.

Mama pulled up her cart. "Now you're going to learn how to protect your garden." She looked at me. "Co-leaders, please come forward."

We both went to her. She took a big roll of netting and two pairs of scissors. "We'll all work together to put this over the plants. That way, the birds can't get to the petals or the fruit."

I took a pair of scissors from Mama. This was

pretty exciting. Usually, we had to watch while the grown-ups did everything.

We cut the netting and then the whole class helped put it over the strawberry plants. I guess this garden was okay, but I suddenly thought about my drawing.

"Why are you looking so sad?" Alexa asked quietly. "Don't you like it?"

"It's nice," I admitted. "But my drawing was better."

"What did it have?"

"A rectangular pond in the middle, just like the Shalimar Gardens," I said dreamily. "And jasmine flowers."

Alexa looked up. "Ooh, I love jasmine!"

"Me too," I replied sadly. "Me too."

12

WORD OF THE DAY

GLORIOUS

Of great beauty

On Friday, Miss Piccolo kept the blinds of our window closed tightly. "You kids get too distracted," she told us. "We need to work, not look outside all day."

"But I need to make sure everything's okay!" I protested.

She shook her head. "The blinds stay closed."

I sighed so loudly, my hair blew away from my face. Alexa crossed her arms on her chest and said, "This is so unfair!"

Miss Piccolo just handed out more rocket math worksheets like it was no big deal.

Suddenly, math wasn't my favorite subject anymore. I think my new favorite subject was gardening.

"Ready for some good news?" Miss Piccolo said.

I looked up. "No homework for a week?" I asked hopefully.

Alexa grinned at me. "Or an ice cream party?"

I had to admit, her idea was way better. I guess I was okay with Alexa R. having good ideas once in a while.

"No," Miss Piccolo said. "It's about the garden. We're having a family day next weekend. We want to show everyone how well you third graders have been working together."

Alexa looked at me.

I looked at Alexa.

"We have a week to make our garden fabulous!" she whispered in my ear.

I nodded firmly. "We can do it. We're co-leaders!"

"And friends?"

I heaved a great big sigh. "Sure."

She squealed. "It will be awesome!"

The news of the family day made the whole class excited. Miss Piccolo emailed invites to all the families and also sent home flyers.

The next week, from Monday to Thursday, everyone did their garden chores without complaining. Even Antonio.

We painted a sign that said WELCOME TO OUR

GARDEN and put it up on the fence near the swings. We even made a scarecrow with a piece of wood and some craft paper. It was creepy and made the birds stay away. So yay!

Everyone listened to me and Alexa. Omar even said, "Aye-aye, Captains!" like we were sailors.

Alexa and I gave each other high fives.

On Friday, I left school early on account of a doctor's appointment. After dinner, I sat with Dadi in her room. We watched an Urdu drama and ate ice cream from plastic bowls. "Your mama will scold us for eating in bed," Dadi told me.

"Aliyah does it all the time," I replied, licking my spoon.

"That doesn't make it right."

"Interesting," I said. "How come when you're older, you can do whatever you want? But I'm the youngest so I have to follow all the rules."

Dadi patted me on the head. "That's not true. And being the youngest is actually a blessing in disguise."

I frowned. "How come?"

"You get help from everyone else," she replied. "Like when you have to clean up your room, your mama always comes in to help you. And when you have homework, your baba always helps you with it. Even Sal and Aliyah help you sometimes."

I thought about it. Sal had fixed my broken Barbie doll more than once. Aliyah was less helpful, but at least I could sneak into her room and *borrow* her stuff. Most of the time, she didn't even find out. "You're right," I finally said. "But still."

Dadi ate some more ice cream. "But nothing. Be grateful for what you have."

I took another bite too. "Okay, I'll try."

"MARYA! GET OVER HERE, QUICK!" Aliyah's shrill voice made me jump.

"Sounds like an emergency," Dadi said, only she was smiling because Aliyah was always super dramatic.

I sighed and went to see what my big sister wanted. Maybe someone threw water on her and she was melting, like the Wicked Witch in Oz. Then I thought of what Dadi had said, and tried to look happy.

This turned out to be a good idea, because Aliyah was in the kitchen, making brownies. "Come help me!" she commanded.

I hurried to get my apron. "Can we make some for my school too?"

She rolled her eyes. "Whatever."

On Saturday morning, my whole family went with me to school. Well, only to the playground, but still. Just so you know, going to school on a weekend was totally weird. Everything was quiet and the parking lot was empty. Even the trucks were gone.

At least we all looked good. Mama wore her best blue hijab, and Dadi wore her favorite polka-dot shalwar kameez. Baba wore a tie like he was going to work. "I'm so proud of you, jaan!" he said.

"Her and the neighbor," Dadi reminded him.

I groaned. "Yes, Alexa too." I didn't want to say that Alexa was a pretty good co-leader, because that would be strange. But it was true.

Sal and Aliyah came with us too, grinning. Well, Sal was grinning. Aliyah wasn't, but at least her mean-face was nowhere to be seen. She was holding a tray of brownies that I'd helped her bake the night before.

We got to the playground. A table with food and water was set up near the benches. There were doughnuts, chips, and apple slices. And lots of juice boxes. I took the tray of brownies from Aliyah and put them right in the center of the table.

Almost everyone's families had come, like Hanna's parents and Antonio's grandparents. Also, Omar's big sister, who was a nurse. Miss Piccolo and Principal Cleveland were also there, talking to each other.

I grinned and waved. Hanna waved back excitedly.

Then I saw Alexa in the corner, standing with her aunt Maryann. That's who usually came to her school events, because Alexa's parents were super busy. I tried not to feel sorry for her, but it was impossible. If Mama and Baba hadn't shown up today, I'd have cried.

"Welcome, families!" Principal Cleveland boomed. He was always booming; it was weird. "We're delighted to show you how hard our third graders have worked to make this project a success."

Everyone clapped. Even Aliyah.

"Co-leaders, please come here!" Miss Piccolo called. I went to stand next to Alexa.

She nudged me and pointed to the garden, which was mostly hidden behind a bunch of grown-ups. "Check it out, Marya."

I frowned because I had no idea what she was talking about. Then the grown-ups moved away, and I gasped.

The garden was glorious! My bird feeder was full of seeds. The flowers were pretty and colorful.

Alexa's gnome sat in the corner, all polished and bright.

Best of all, there was a little rectangular pond in the center of the garden. "It's just a container with water," Alexa explained. "But it works, doesn't it?"

I nodded very fast. "It totally does!"

My family came to stand next to me. "This is just like Shalimar Gardens!" Baba said in a shocked voice.

I still couldn't believe it. "How? When?" I sputtered.

"It was my idea," Alexa said shyly. "Hanna and Miss Piccolo helped on Friday, after you went to the doctor."

My mouth opened and closed like a fish. "Seriously?"

She shrugged. "Well, your drawing was pretty cool."

I couldn't help it. In a surprise move, I turned and hugged Alexa. "This is fabulous!" I whispered. "Thank you."

She blushed. "You're welcome, co-leader."

I groaned as I let her go, but I was joking. Mostly. I actually didn't mind being co-leader anymore. It was nice to share the responsibility with someone else.

Dadi nudged me. "Look, my favorite flower."

I leaned closer to see where she pointed. Sure enough, there was a whole row of delicate white flowers in the back of the garden. "Jasmine!" I said.

Okay, I yelled.

I turned to Alexa, who was grinning widely. "I begged your mom to order these last time she was here."

I sputtered, because apparently my mama and my archenemy were now best friends? Only I looked at Alexa's face and realized she wasn't really my archenemy.

Maybe.

Possibly.

Then I looked around my garden, like Queen Marya at her kingdom. Jasmine flowers made my garden totally fabulous.

Now it's your turn! Finish the garden plan and color it in, either below or by tracing it onto a sheet of paper.

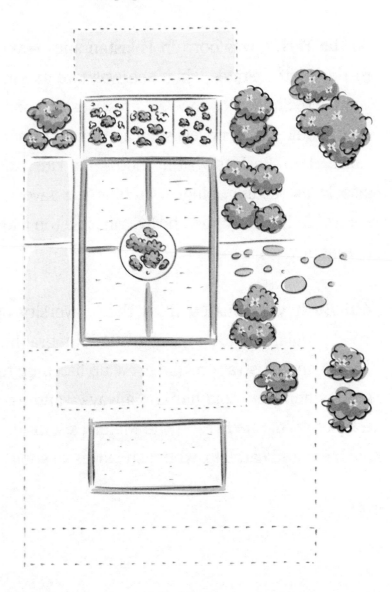

ABOUT THE AUTHOR
AND ILLUSTRATOR

Saadia Faruqi was born in Pakistan and moved to the United States when she was twenty-two years old. She writes the Yasmin series and popular middle-grade novels such as *Yusuf Azeem Is Not a Hero*. Besides writing books for kids, she also loves reading, binge-watching her favorite shows, and taking naps. She lives in Houston with her family.

Ani Bushry graduated from the University of West England with a background in graphic design and illustration. She grew up listening to stories her mom told her and always wanted to tell her own. She lives in the Maldives with her husband and cat, Lilo, whom she loves to spoil.